FRANKIE'S
MAGIC
FOOTBALL

BY FRANK LAMPARD

METEOR MADNESS
FRANK LAMPARD

LITTLE, BROWN BOOKS FOR YOUNG READERS
www.lbkids.co.uk

LITTLE, BROWN BOOKS FOR YOUNG READERS

First published in Great Britain in 2015 by Hodder & Stoughton

1 3 5 7 9 10 8 6 4 2

A CIP catalogue record for this book
is available from the British Library.

ISBN 978-0-349-13207-5

Typeset in Cantarell by M Rules
Printed and bound in Great Britain by
Clays Ltd, St Ives plc

The paper and board used in this book are
made from wood from responsible sources.

MIX
Paper from
responsible sources
FSC® C104740

Little, Brown Books for Young Readers
An imprint of
Hachette Children's Group
Part of Hodder & Stoughton
Carmelite House
50 Victoria Embankment
London EC4Y 0DZ

An Hachette UK Company
www.hachette.co.uk

www.lbkids.co.uk

*To my mum Pat, who encouraged
me to do my homework in between
kicking a ball all around the house,
and is still with me every
step of the way.*

Welcome to a fantastic Fantasy League – the greatest football competition ever held in this world or any other!

You'll need four on a team, so choose carefully. This is a lot more serious than a game in the park. You'll never know who your next opponents will be, or where you'll face them.

So lace up your boots, players, and good luck! The whistle's about to blow!

The Ref

CHAPTER 1

Bright sunshine trickled through the leaves of the forest as Frankie and his family pulled up next to a log cabin.

"The holiday officially starts here!" announced Frankie's dad.

"Just what we need," his mum

said, opening the car door. "Some time with Mother Nature."

Kevin looked up from his games console. "Yeah, great," he grumbled. "Loads of insects and a lumpy bed."

Frankie unclipped his seat belt, and jumped out of the car. They'd been driving for nearly three hours to reach the holiday camp. Max whined from the back, so Frankie went to let him out too. He sprang out on to the grass.

Frankie breathed in the crisp air of the forest. He couldn't wait to explore the camp. Apparently there were tennis courts, an outdoor heated pool and even a mini theme park. But the best thing about this whole trip was that Louise and Charlie were coming with their families as well.

"Hey, Frankie, give me a hand with the luggage, will you?" asked his dad.

Frankie saw his father struggling with a huge suitcase, and rushed over to help him. Together, they dragged it out of the car. Frankie's football rolled out after it.

"I don't know why you keep that old thing," said his dad. "Didn't we get you a new ball for your last birthday?"

Frankie grinned and picked up

the battered, half-deflated ball. His dad didn't know that the football had magic powers that could take them on amazing adventures.

"Yeah, Frankenstein," said Kevin, smirking. "Why don't you just throw it away?"

Kevin knew all about the football's powers. Frankie didn't trust him with the secret one bit.

"I guess I'm just attached to it," he mumbled.

Frankie's mum had unlocked the door to the cabin, and they began to carry all their luggage inside. Frankie took his bag, and the ball, into a room with a bunk bed.

"I'm having the top!" said Kevin, shoving him out of the way and heaving his rucksack on to the top mattress.

"Fine," said Frankie, with a sigh.

As he went back into the living room, he saw his dad carrying a long black case he'd never seen before.

"What's that?" he asked.

His dad smiled as he laid it carefully on the table. He clicked open the lid. Inside, cushioned in padding, was a telescope.

"Goodness!" said Frankie's mum, peering over his shoulder. "Have you still got that?"

"I dug it out of the loft," said his

dad. Frankie watched as he took out and unfolded a tripod. "I used it years ago, for looking at the stars. There are too many street lights where we live now."

"Boring," said Kevin. "Who wants to look at the stars?"

"Actually," Frankie's dad said, "there's supposed to be a meteor shower tonight. If it stays clear, it should be quite a sight."

Max started barking, and Frankie went to the front door. Louise and Charlie were rushing along the path.

"Hi guys," said Frankie. "You're here already!"

"We're in the next cabins along," said Louise, tickling Max's chin. "Isn't this place amazing?"

"Yeah, great," grumbled Kevin.

"Ignore him," said Frankie. "Have you explored yet?"

"We were waiting for you," said Charlie.

Frankie's dad was putting away the telescope. "Why don't you all go for a swim while your mum and I unpack?" he said.

"No can do," said Charlie, holding up his hands. He was wearing his goalie gloves. "Can't get these wet."

Frankie's mum arrived. "Well, you could . . . take them off?"

Frankie and Louise laughed. Sometimes parents said the funniest things! Charlie never took his gloves off. He even wore them to bed.

Frankie whistled for Max. The little dog came scampering from a bush.

"You coming, Kev?" asked Frankie.

His brother shrugged. "I'd rather stay here and finish my game."

Suit yourself, Frankie thought.

He set off into the camp with his friends, then remembered something. He dashed back and grabbed his magic football. No way was he leaving it with Kevin.

There were paths leading

around the holiday camp, and maps showing where all the attractions were. There were lots of other kids around with their parents and several dogs as well. People were climbing trees, eating on fold-out tables, and playing with Frisbees and badminton rackets.

They passed loads of other cabins, the tennis courts and a restaurant, until at last they saw a roller coaster track peeking above the trees. The theme park!

"Wow, cool!" said Frankie. "Let's check it out."

They followed the track to a set of gates, with a sign made out of looping metal letters. *World of Wonder*, it said.

Beneath it was another sign, written in red pen: *Closed Until Further Notice*.

The gate suddenly opened and a man in blue overalls came out.

"Sorry, kids," he said. "There's been some sort of electrical fault. None of the rides have any power."

Frankie's heart sagged. "Oh."

"But I see you're footballers," said the maintenance man, nodding to the ball under Frankie's arm. "There's a five-a-side pitch just round the corner." He pointed at the path.

"Yay!" said Louise, her eyes lighting up. "Let's go." The three of them ran up the path, with Max following.

Soon Frankie had forgotten all about his disappointment. They had the whole pitch to themselves, but he thought it wouldn't take long to find other visitors who wanted to play as well.

"Perhaps we can organise a tournament," said Charlie, as he dived to stop another shot.

"Great idea!" said Frankie. "But we only have four players, and that's if we include Max."

"What about your brother?"

asked Louise. She kicked the ball to Frankie.

"We'll have to prise him away from his console first," he said, as he lined up the ball for a curling shot.

Max let out a sudden bark, and Frankie fluffed his kick. The ball curled off at an angle, sailing high into the air. Max was hopping around the bottom of a tree, while a squirrel watched from a branch above.

"Max, you put me off!" said Frankie.

Max lowered his head.

"Where'd the ball go?" said Charlie.

Then they all heard a beeping sound. It was coming from over the wall, where the theme park was.

"Weird," said Louise. "I thought that man said the electrics were down?"

"Perhaps it's up and running

again!" said Frankie. "Let's go and look."

He ran back around to the main gate, which was slightly ajar.

"Are you sure about this?" said Louise.

"We're just going in to get the ball," said Frankie.

Still, he cast a nervous glance back as he pushed through the gate. Everything was still, apart from some coloured lights flashing further into the park. Frankie's skin tingled. Had the power come back on? Or was this the work of the magic football? It wouldn't be the first time it had made strange things happen.

Most of the rides were silent. He saw a roller coaster, a clown's circus, a ghost house and several others. The flashing lights were coming from a model space shuttle supported by a long beam. Frankie guessed it swung up and down. The ride was called "Galaxy Quest".

But he couldn't see the ball anywhere.

Max trotted up to the spaceship and sniffed around. Then he rested his paws on it.

"I think he's smelled something," said Frankie. Leaning over the spaceship's edge, he saw the ball lodged under one of the seats. "It's here!" Frankie jumped up into the ride.

"Cool!" said Charlie, climbing up as well. "I've always wanted to be an astronaut! One small save for man, one giant save for—"

He went quiet as the ride creaked into motion, swinging slowly forwards on the long arm. Frankie stumbled backwards on to one of the seats.

"Er . . . is it supposed to do that?" said Louise. "Maybe I should go and get someone."

The ride rocked backwards again. Frankie saw the ball was glowing a little.

"I think it's the magic of the football," he said. "It must want us to go. Quick, climb in!"

Louise grabbed Max and passed him to Frankie as the spaceship swung back and forth. Then she scrambled in herself. "Fasten your seatbelts!" she cried.

The ride moved faster, swinging high into the air. Frankie's stomach yo-yoed up and down, but he pulled down the harness bars over his head until they clicked into place. He held Max in his lap.

"Do you think it's safe?" Charlie shouted.

"I trust the football!" said Frankie, as the shuttle rocked higher.

The spaceship swooped downwards, then climbed up the other side. This time it didn't stop and swung upside-down, before plummeting again. "It's getting faster!" shouted Louise.

The forest and the other rides shot past as the spaceship dipped and rose in huge circles. Frankie wondered if he'd made a mistake. What if the ride was actually dangerous?

He saw smoke coming from the arm that held the rocket.

"We should get off!" cried Charlie.

Sparks fizzed in all directions. Then, with a few pops, the bolts and screws exploded. The whole ride began to shake. "It's falling to bits!" yelled Louise. Max was trembling on Frankie's knee, and he held him tight. They spun faster and faster, until everything was a blur.

Then as the rocket rose again, Frankie felt it lurch. With a horrible tear of metal, they shot into the sky.

CHAPTER 2

"We're . . . flying!" gasped Louise.

Frankie saw the campsite disappearing below. The trees and the cabins looked like something from a model village, and beyond he could see a lake, and roads, and fields. But he realised something else — he couldn't feel the wind.

There was now a see-through shield over the rocket, protecting them. And all the buttons at the front were flashing, as though they really worked. There was a steering column, too. He let go of Max and gripped it.

"The ride has turned into a real shuttle!" he said.

Charlie placed his gloves against the glass shield. "Yes, but where are we flying to?"

Frankie saw the world shrink even more. Now he could see mountains and huge cities, sparkling with light. Then the coast. And the sea!

"I guess space shuttles go into space, right?" said Max in a gruff voice. Whenever the football worked its magic, Frankie's dog could talk.

Flames shot out of the back of the rocket, and the sky outside was getting blacker by the second. Thousands of stars pinpricked the sky. "You said you always wanted to be an astronaut, Charlie. Well, your wish has come true!"

Max started floating off his lap. Frankie felt himself become weightless in his seat as well.

"Help, catch me!" Max barked.

"There's no gravity," said Louise.

She unclipped her safety harness and did a somersault mid-air.

"I've got to try that too!" said Charlie. He pushed off from his seat, and spread his arms, flying like a plane over Frankie's head.

Max bounced off the glass shield, paws scrabbling in the empty air upside-down. "I don't like it. Dogs aren't supposed to be in space."

"Actually, the first creature in space was a dog," said Louise. "She was called Laika, from Russia!"

"Wow — you know everything," said Charlie. Frankie smiled to see Louise blush.

He gently took hold of Max's collar, and turned him upright. He tried to work out what all the controls could be. One said "Blasters", another read "Shields" and a third was labelled "Artificial Gravity".

"Perhaps this will help," he said, pressing it.

With a succession of thumps, his three friends fell back into their seats. "Ouch!" said Charlie, rubbing his head. "You could have warned me."

Frankie's bottom rested on the seat again. Louise was laughing. "I thought you were always ready, Charlie," she said. Then she pointed out into space. "Oh, wow!"

Frankie turned. A blue-and-green sphere floated against the blackness of deep space. Wisps of cloud swirled over its surface. It was planet Earth!

"I wonder what this button does," said Max. He reached out a paw and pressed a red button on the control panel. Two laser bolts shot from the front of the ship, disappearing into space.

Frankie batted his paw away. "Don't fiddle!"

Suddenly, there was a crackle of

static that made them all jump, and a voice filled the spaceship.

"Unidentified craft, we have detected you. State your name and purpose."

Frankie realised the question was coming from the control panel.

"What do we say?" asked Charlie.

"I repeat: state your name and purpose."

There was a button on the panel that read "Comms".

Frankie pressed it. "Er . . . we're . . . we're just . . ."

Louise leant over his shoulder. "We're the Galaxy Quest," she said. "Who are you?"

There was another crackle. "We're the MW1274 Space Station. You're about to crash into us."

Frankie gripped the controls as the black section of space in front of them shimmered. A huge structure like a spinning doughnut appeared. It had antennae bristling over its surface, as well as satellite dishes and hundreds of portholes. They were heading right towards it!

Frankie turned the steering column hard to the side and the rocket's nose jerked right.

"It's not enough!" cried Charlie.

They were flying straight at the side of the space station. Max covered his eyes with a paw.

Frankie gritted his teeth, and pulled harder on the column. *We might just make it . . .*

CRUNCH! The ship jerked as its underside hit a satellite dish. Lots of alarms went off and lights flashed across the bank of controls.

Frankie pressed the Comms button again. He couldn't think what to say, so he just said "Sorry!"

"Galaxy Quest, please proceed to Docking Bay Four. You have some explaining to do."

Red lights appeared across one

side of the space station, flashing arrows towards an opening.

"I guess that's Docking Bay Four," said Louise.

Frankie steered the craft towards it. But they were still going too fast. "Any idea where the brakes are?" he said.

As they came close, a beam shone out of the docking bay, surrounding their ship. Frankie tried to steer, but it had no effect. The beam was sucking them in. The ship entered the opening and came to rest on a metal platform. Then the doors swished closed behind them, blocking out the view of Earth, now like a distant football drifting in space.

Frankie pressed a button that read "Cockpit Release" and the glass shield hissed open.

"Suddenly home seems a long way off," said Charlie.

A buzzing noise made them all snap their heads around. A little robot on four legs trotted into the hangar. It looked a lot like a dog, with a wagging antenna for a tail and flashing green eyes. "About two thousand miles, actually," it said.

Max barked, leaping out of the rocket. Frankie climbed out after

him. He left the magic football
inside. Max sniffed at the robot.

"You know, I've waited a long
time to find another talking dog,"
he said.

"I am not a dog," said the robot.
"I'm Lieutenant Wagalot, a canine
droid with more power in my nose

circuits than in your most advanced supercomputer."

Max licked its metallic face. "Yeah, but I bet you like chasing sticks, don't you?"

Wagalot turned up its snout and spun on its heels. "Please follow me," it said.

As the robot sped off, Frankie looked at Louise and Charlie, and shrugged. "I guess we don't have much choice," he said.

They trailed through an automatic door into a pristine white corridor that followed a gentle curve. Frankie guessed it went the entire loop of the structure.

"What is this place?" called Charlie.

"Your questions will be answered soon," the robot told him.

They passed several other doorways. All of them were closed, but through their glass viewing windows Frankie caught sight of classrooms full of chairs and tables, a swimming pool, a gymnasium with weights and machines, and what looked like a small cinema.

Then they heard chanting coming their way.

"*We are fit, and we are keen!*
Intergalactic defence machine!"

The robot sidestepped as several

people came jogging along the corridor. Frankie jumped back in shock. The person at the front of the line had two heads!

One head carried on the chant, "No sun too hot, no planet too far!" and the other replied, "To boldly fly up to the stars!"

Both faces gave Frankie and his friends a puzzled look. "Weird," said the one on the left. "Imagine having only one head," said the right.

Behind him came what looked like a giant ant, its feelers twitching. Max hid behind Frankie's legs. Coming up behind the ant was a strange globule of slime, shimmering different colours as it wobbled along the corridor. It didn't seem to have any arms or legs, but a tentacle stuck out from the top with a single eye at the tip. The last in the line was some sort of centipede ten metres long, with a wide grinning mouth. The only thing they all had in common was that they were wearing a red uniform.

"No way!" one of the creatures said. "I didn't think humans were real."

The globule's eye swivelled back. "I didn't realise they were so ugly," it said, in a gurgling voice.

As they disappeared around the bend, Charlie's eyes grew wide. "Did that thing call me ugly?" he asked.

"Wait here, please," said the robotic dog. It raised up on its rear paws, perfectly balanced, and a ray shone from its front paw on to a pad on the wall. The walls on both sides shot past while the floor stayed still. A door came to a stop beside them.

"Enter!" boomed a voice.

Lieutenant Wagalot dropped on to four paws again. "Good luck," it said. Then it added in a quiet voice, "You'll need it."

CHAPTER 3

The door opened and Frankie
led the way inside. The air was
hot and misty, and the room was
filled with green plants. Huge fern
leaves sprouted from the walls and
creepers hung from the ceiling.
Exotic flowers of every colour
bloomed from the floor. "Come in,"

croaked a voice, "before you let all the heat out."

Once everyone was inside, the doors closed behind them.

Frankie pushed forwards past a looping vine. He reached a pool of murky green water. In the centre was a huge leathery lily pad, and on it sat the biggest frog he'd ever seen. It was wearing a tight-fitting red uniform over its bulging limbs, and watched them with bulbous eyes. Large flies buzzed lazily through the air.

"It's normal to salute in front of your commanding officer," the frog said.

Frankie managed to give a salute. "Sorry, sir," he mumbled.

"That's better!" said the frog. "But it's ma'am, actually."

"Sorry, ma'am," they all said together.

"I am Commander Greb," said the frog. "You must be the new recruits."

"Actually, we . . ." Frankie began.

"Well, you're late," said Commander Greb. "And you destroyed a satellite on the way in. Not a good start, is it? I don't know how any of you hope to win the Cadet Medal flying like that!"

Frankie's ears pricked up. "What's the Cadet Medal?"

The Commander frowned. "It's the trophy for most promising astronaut student!" she said. "Are you sure you should be here?" She took out a clipboard and studied it. "I'm not sure I have any Earthlings on my register . . ."

"Oh, we're supposed to be

here!" said Frankie. Charlie nudged him, looking puzzled, so Frankie lowered his voice to a whisper. "The football always sets us a challenge," he said. "We must have to win this medal."

"Good thinking," said Louise.

"Well, you'd better keep out of trouble from now ..." Suddenly a bell sounded, making them all jump. "Ah, lunchtime!" said the Commander. Her tongue shot out, unfurling across the room and wrapping around an unlucky fly. She gobbled it up.

"Yuck!" said Max. "I don't like flies for lunch."

"Don't be silly," said the Commander. "You need to head to the canteen with all the other cadets. Off you go, and stay out of trouble from now on!"

Back out in the corridor, the robotic dog was waiting for them.

"How do we get to the canteen?" asked Louise.

Lieutenant Wagalot pointed a paw. "One hundred and fourteen doors on your right."

"Can you do that thing where the door comes to us?" said Charlie.

"Negative," said the dog. "That's for ranking officers only."

*

They marched along the corridor together. "How are we going to win this medal?" said Charlie. "We don't know the first thing about space."

"You've always wanted to be an astronaut," said Frankie. "This is your chance."

They knew they'd reached the canteen from the hubbub of voices and clashing plates. As the doors automatically opened, they saw lots of tables. All sorts of different aliens were sitting on the benches. Some looked almost human but had a different number of arms, or heads, or legs. Others looked like slugs, or plants, or insects, or like the slime creature they'd seen in the corridor earlier. A red-shelled beetle the size of a sheep was munching on some sort of cabbage. It looked up at them, its face covered in green mush, then carried on eating.

"Gross!" said Charlie. "I've lost my appetite."

Frankie saw a stack of trays in a hole in the wall and glanced around, looking for some sort of food counter, but he couldn't see one. His stomach grumbled. The slime ball had grown another tentacle and dipped it into a bowl of brown gunge, sucking it up.

"I'd kill for a slice of pizza," said Louise.

"With ham and pineapple?" said a voice.

Louise glanced around. "Who said that?"

This time the recess with the trays glowed a pale blue. "Perhaps you prefer plain cheese and tomato?"

"Do you have pepperoni?" asked Charlie.

"Affirmative." Several beams of light shone on to the top tray and a slice of steaming pizza appeared out of thin air.

"Woohoo!" said Charlie, grabbing the tray. He breathed in deeply.

"That's what I call service. It smells amazing!"

"Can I have mushroom, please?" asked Louise.

A slice of mushroom pizza appeared on the next tray.

After she'd taken it, Frankie said, "How about a burger? No! A cheeseburger ..."

Instantly, a fat cheeseburger arrived on the tray. Frankie's mouth watered as he picked it up.

He looked around for somewhere to sit.

"Ahem!" said Max from near his ankles. "Are we forgetting someone?"

"Sorry, boy!" said Frankie. "Any chance of a bone please?"

"Extra juicy if possible," Max added.

The bone appeared.

Once Frankie had given his dog the bone, they went in search of a seat. Several of the aliens viewed them with narrowed eyes, or what Frankie thought were eyes. The boy with two heads shifted along his bench to make room for them, and the centipede scuttled out of the way too.

"Thanks," said Frankie, sitting down.

"No problem," said both heads.

Then one started eating some sort of spaghetti. "Our name is Bix, by the way," said the one who wasn't eating.

"Frankie," said Frankie. "And these are my friends Charlie, Louise and Max."

Charlie picked up the pizza in his gloves and took a big bite. Melted cheese dribbled down his chin. "This is the best pizza ever!" he said. "That machine is incredible."

"Just a standard molecular sustenance generator," said the right head.

"They'd never be able to find a chef to please so many different species," said the left. "Some of these aliens have disgusting tastes."

Frankie sank his teeth into his burger, and the flavour burst over his tongue. Charlie was right – this wasn't just any burger, it was a perfect burger.

"So," said Louise turning to the centipede. "We're from Earth. What planet are you from?"

The centipede sneezed.

"Bless you," said Louise.

The alien boy laughed. "No, that's where Terri's from. It's hard to pronounce."

"Ah," said Charlie. He nodded to the centipede. "Hi, Terri."

"And you?" asked Frankie.

"Vega system," said Bix. "About three light years from your planet. Everyone here is from the Milky Way galaxy. How come you only arrived today?"

Frankie and his friends glanced at each other. He sensed the magic football might be a long story, so he thought of something quickly. "Our ship's engine needed work."

"Well, you've got some catching up to do if you want to win the Cadet Medal," said the boy.

Louise had finished her pizza. "So how do you get this medal?" she said.

"You have to come top in all the different subjects," said Bix. "PE, astrophysics theory, space engineering and flight school."

Frankie grimaced. How could they ever do that? He didn't know the first thing about astrophysics or engineering! And if they failed, would they ever make it home?

The bell rang again and all the students began to stand, slither, or crawl from their seats.

"It's PE!" said Bix. "Our favourite."

Phew! thought Frankie. *At least that's one subject I can do.*

"How about your crew play my

team?" said Bix. He paused. "That's if you're any good at football?"

Frankie grinned. *Even better!*

Charlie smacked his gloves together. "Let's do it," he said.

Everyone filed out of the canteen and into the corridor. Frankie watched as lots of alien cadets took various doors into other rooms. He stayed close to Bix and Terri. On the way, the slimeball introduced himself as Gloop, and the ant said her name was QuiggQuiggQuigg.

Bix led them into a dark room, then said "Lights!"

White light lit up the interior.

The room was a perfect cube with bare walls, apart from two circular goal-nets on opposite walls. But something wasn't right. For some reason the floor was padded like a trampoline. Plus, the goals weren't at ground level – they were halfway up the walls!

"Erm . . . I don't think I can save anything that high," Charlie muttered to Frankie.

"Ball, please," said Bix. A hatch opened in the wall and a football rolled out into the middle of the pitch. At least that looked normal.

"Ready?" said Terri.

Frankie shrugged. "I guess so."

It might look a bit different, but he was still confident they could win.

"Switch off the AG," said the centipede alien.

"AG?" said Frankie, just as his tummy felt funny and the soles of his feet drifted off the ground.

"Artificial gravity!" said Louise, floating away beside him.

Gloop pushed off the floor towards one of the goals.

"You said you'd played before. That's right, isn't it?" said Bix.

"Yes!" said Frankie. *But not like this . . .*

CHAPTER 4

Bix kicked the ball through the air. Louise tried to intercept, but ended up spinning helplessly until she bumped into the far wall.

"We can't be losing already," Frankie muttered.

Terri looped her centipede tail and flicked the ball through Max's legs. Quigg the ant caught it and headed towards the goal. Charlie scrambled after the ball, flailing in mid-air, but didn't get to it in time. The net ballooned as the ball hit it.

Charlie fished the ball out of the back of the net. Louise pushed off the ceiling and joined Frankie, floating in the middle of the room. Max's paws were scrabbling in the air as he slowly drifted towards them. Frankie caught him by the collar.

"This isn't anything like a normal football game," said Frankie.

"No kidding," shouted Charlie.

"I haven't felt this sick since I ate

that snail from the garden," Max said.

"Up, down, left and right don't matter in here," said Louise, turning over in a slow somersault. "If you need to move, you have to push off something and drift. That's what they do – look!"

Frankie glanced across at the other team. They were all sitting on a wall or on the ceiling, apart from Gloop who was clinging with a tentacle to one of the goalposts.

"Got it!" said Charlie. "Okay team, spread out."

Still holding Max, Frankie pushed off against Louise. She drifted to the ceiling, and he floated to the floor. Or perhaps it was the other way around. With no gravity, he couldn't tell any more. Then he placed Max down. "Ready, boy?"

Max wagged his tail. "Let's show them what Earthlings are made of!"

Charlie hurled the ball underarm towards Louise. Bix leapt towards it, but Louise pushed herself forwards too. She reached it a fraction before the two-headed boy, blocking the ball with her foot. Bix tripped over her leg and went spinning.

Louise, knocked upside-down, kicked it over her head into the middle of the chamber. Terri snaked across the pitch, but Frankie extended his leg in a sliding airborne tackle, snatching it from her.

He came out with the ball at his feet. Quigg the giant ant was shooting along beneath him. She suddenly spread a set of transparent wings and changed direction towards Frankie. He gripped the ball between his feet and somersaulted past her. He couldn't stop himself spinning, though. The goal appeared in his line of sight, then disappeared as he rolled over and over. He was getting dizzy. Gloop was bobbing in the centre of the goal, tentacles spread out.

"That's not fair!" he heard Charlie cry.

Frankie flicked the ball towards the goal, but his shot had no power. Gloop reached with a tentacle and batted it away.

"Great save!" shouted Bix.

Frankie hit a wall and steadied himself, then turned to see a shape darting across the chamber. It was Louise, arms tucked close to her sides. She headed the ball and sent it flying back towards the goal. This time Gloop wasn't quick enough and the ball crashed into the goal.

Louise flipped herself over,
planting her feet against the wall.

Frankie clapped and Max yapped
happily.

"That was amazing, Lou!"
shouted Charlie.

Their friend blushed.

"You guys are good!" said Bix. "I

heard Earthlings never even had a team in the lowest galactic league before, but you should definitely enter."

"How about next goal wins?" said Frankie. His blood was pumping.

"Sure," said Bix, both faces grinning. "We won't go easy, though."

"We won't either!" said Max, panting.

Each team took their positions on the walls again. "Ready?" said Gloop. He clutched the ball in a tentacle and drew it back.

But before he could throw it, the whole room shook with a rumbling sound.

"What was that?" said Quigg, feelers twitching.

"All cadets to the control room!" said Commander Greb's voice over the speakers. "Emergency procedure! I repeat: all cadets to the control room."

The room shook again and Frankie heard what sounded like a distant explosion.

Louise's face had turned pale.

"It's probably just a drill," Bix said, but there was a tremor in his voice. "Activate AG!" he added. Gloop sank to the ground and laid a squishy hand on the button.

Frankie suddenly felt incredibly

heavy. He fell with a cry, tumbling through the air with everyone else. He thumped into the padded floor, bounced, then landed again. "So that's why it's padded!" said Max, scrambling on to his paws. "For when the gravity kicks in."

They all rushed out into the corridor where other cadets were gathering.

"Follow me," said Bix.

Another quake flung everyone off their feet.

"What's happening?" said Louise, helping Charlie up.

Lieutenant Wagalot galloped past. "Please stay calm," it said.

"We appear to be in the midst of a meteor shower."

"A drill meteor shower?" asked Charlie.

The robotic dog cocked its head. "I'm afraid not."

With the space station rocking, they staggered after Bix to a door. It opened to reveal an enormous room lined with monitors and flashing control panels. Red lights glowed across the ceiling. Commander Greb was sitting in a large chair, staring at a screen that looked out over space. Frankie saw hundreds of meteors streaking past. Some were just football sized, but others were as big as cars!

"The hull is holding," said the commander as the ship shook again. "As long as we don't get anything bigger than this, we should be . . . Oh! Oh no."

"What?" said Charlie.

Lieutenant Wagalot tapped at one of the monitors. The robot's tail drooped. "We're picking up a rather large meteor," it said. "Two hundred and twelve metres across, to be precise. It'll hit in less than two minutes."

Frankie swallowed. "Can the hull stand up to a meteor that big?"

Commander Greb's face turned a deeper shade of green. Frankie gulped. "I'm guessing the answer is 'no'," he whispered.

"There must be something we can do," Louise said.

Lieutenant Wagalot stabbed at the control panel. "Our escape pods are not working," it said. "Damaged by the shower."

"Can't you shoot down the meteor?" said Charlie.

"If we had weapons, we could," said the commander, "but this is just a cadet training station. We're not armed."

An idea flickered in Frankie's

brain. The space station might not be armed, but he knew a ship that was.

"The Galaxy Quest!" he said, remembering the buttons on the control panel. "It has blasters. We could fly out there and stop the meteor!"

"I've seen your flying, cadet," said Lieutenant Wagalot. "You'll never make it."

"It's got a point," muttered Charlie.

Louise put her hand on his shoulder. "Frankie's right. We thought we came here to win the Cadet Medal, but what if the football actually brought us here to save the space station?"

"Football? Look, I don't know what you're talking about," said Commander Greb, "but you're our only chance. Show them to their ship, Lieutenant." The giant frog saluted them. So did the rest of the cadets, before quickly running to hide under desks.

Frankie and his crew saluted back.

"We won't fail you," said Frankie.

As he followed the robotic dog from the room, he hoped he was right.

CHAPTER 5

The Galaxy Quest was still where they'd left it in Docking Bay Four. Frankie leapt into the front seat, with Max hopping on to his lap, and the others jumped in too. Every few seconds a new impact shook the space station.

Charlie held out a hand, gloved

fingers splayed in a V-shape. "Live long and prosper, Lieutenant," he said.

"Pardon?" said the dog droid.

"May the Force be with you?" said Charlie.

Lieutenant Wagalot shook its head. "You're not making any sense."

"Never mind," said Charlie. He pulled down the cockpit shield.

"Be careful," said the lieutenant. "If even a small meteor hits you, that's it!"

Frankie grimaced. It reminded him of a game he used to play with Kevin, when he'd have to run the length of the garden without being hit by a football. Only this time it was life or death. They needed to destroy that meteor before it hit the station.

As the docking door opened, the platform with the craft on rotated until it faced out into space. Frankie gasped. Meteors shot past. Bits of metal and stray antennae floated in front of the doorway. Frankie rested his hands on the controls. *Come on, you can do it*, he told himself. Then he hit the thrusters. With a *whoosh!* their ship shot out into the deadly hail of rock and debris.

"Look out!" cried Louise.

Frankie steered the shuttle over a streaking meteor. He banked sideways as another flew past, barely missing them.

Frankie kept his eyes peeled, dodging left and right, up and down as he flew the shuttle right into the centre of the meteor shower. It was like dodging defenders who were trying to tackle him!

Commander Greb's voice came over the speakers. "Thirty seconds to impact — you should be able to see the meteor soon."

"There it is," said Charlie in a low voice. Frankie had never seen anything like it — it looked like a mountain shooting through space. His palms were suddenly slick with sweat. He lined up the craft and pressed the blaster trigger. Laser bolts streaked ahead, crashing into the side of the meteor. Apart from a few puffs of dust, they seemed to have no effect.

"Twenty seconds to impact!" croaked the commander. "You have to hit it right in the centre. Our scanners indicate it's the weakest point."

"You can do it, Frankie!" said Louise from behind him.

Frankie narrowed his eyes and

fired again. Cracks spread across the huge mass of rock, but the meteor stormed towards their ship, unstoppable.

"Ten seconds!"

The meteor filled the view ahead. Frankie felt like an ant about to be squashed.

"We're going to crash right into it," said Charlie. Max was trembling in the seat beside Frankie.

He took a deep breath and pulled the trigger again. The lasers streaked right into the heart of the meteor.

The ball of rock exploded into smithereens, scattering fragments

on every side. Small pieces of rock peppered the Galaxy Quest as it flew through the blast, but Frankie gripped the controls and kept it steady.

"Hooray!" cried Frankie's friends.

"You did it!" said Commander Greb. "You saved the station! All four of you will be awarded the Cadet Medal."

Frankie's heart swelled as he steered the ship in a loop the loop. Then he turned it to face back towards the space station. The magic football still glowed on the floor of the shuttle.

Another match won! thought Frankie.

Then the craft juddered. The control panel sparked and all the lights went off.

"Uh-oh," said Charlie.

The nose of the vessel began to tip. Frankie pulled back on the steering column, but nothing happened.

"The engines are dead!" said Louise. "They must have been damaged by debris."

The Galaxy Quest began to tumble through space, back towards Earth.

"Hang on!" Frankie warned everyone.

They fell faster and faster. The sky turned from black to indigo as they entered the Earth's atmosphere. Frankie felt himself pressed back against his seat as the tip of the ship glowed orange, then red hot.

"We're going to crash!" said Charlie.

They tore through clouds. Below, Frankie saw the outline of green land in a dark blue sea. He saw mountain ranges and reservoirs and patchwork fields, then roads and rivers threading across the landscape. Charlie scrambled over the back of his seat.

"There must be something we can do!" he said. He pressed every switch on the control panel, but nothing slowed their descent.

"What about that lever?" barked Max over the whistling rush of the wind outside.

"What lever?" everyone yelled.

Max pointed a paw at a lever just beside the front seat. There was a picture of an umbrella on it.

"Can't hurt!" shouted Charlie. He wrapped his gloved fingers around it and yanked hard.

Frankie heard a bang behind him and something white exploded from the back of the shuttle.

Not an umbrella! Frankie realised. *A parachute.*

He felt a jolt around his shoulders as the parachute ballooned open, slowing the shuttle instantly.

They drifted down towards a forest.

"It's the holiday camp!" said Louise.

Frankie saw that she was right.
There were cabins and tennis courts
among the trees. He spotted the
football pitch and the theme park.
They fell right towards it, nose first,
faster than he would have liked.

"Hang on, everyone!" he
shouted, as the ground rushed to
meet them.

Thump!

They all fell forwards in their
safety harnesses, then the back end
of the ship toppled to the ground as
well, shaking Frankie to his bones.
Smoke trailed from the shuttle's
engines. The cockpit shield slid
back and Frankie sucked in a deep

sigh of relief, enjoying the clean forest air.

"Hey!" said a voice. "What are you up to?"

Frankie's head whipped round. The man in the blue overalls was standing at the gate to the theme park, with a toolbox in his hand. He looked cross.

"I ... er ... we ..." Louise mumbled.

"We lost our football over the wall," said Frankie, plucking the ball from near his feet and holding it up.

"Well, get on your way," said the maintenance man, his face softening. "You shouldn't really be in here." He ducked out of sight again, speaking into a walkie-talkie. "No, it's just kids. Nothing to worry about."

Frankie and his friends clambered from the space shuttle, which now looked exactly as it had before they went on their adventure. The sky was almost completely black above.

"Mum and Dad will be wondering where I am!" he said.

As he walked towards the gate, he passed close to the entrance to the runaway train ride. Frankie felt the ball vibrate in his hands, and one of the train cars seemed to shift slightly, with a hissing sound. He stopped.

"Did you see that?" he said.

Louise and Charlie nodded.

Frankie grinned. "My guess is that the ball can bring all the rides to life," he said. "Cool!"

"Cool?" said Charlie. "We almost got flattened by a giant meteor!"

"Yes, but we saved the station," said Frankie. "The ball must want us to help in other ways too!" He thought about Bix and the other aliens, still up in space. It was a shame they'd never get to finish their football game.

Louise smiled. "This time tomorrow, then?"

Frankie nodded, Max barked, and Charlie shrugged. "I'll be ready," he said.

"You're always ready!" said Louise.

By the time Frankie and Max had run back to their cabin, his mum was clearing away plates from a table outside. Kevin lounged on a chair, still playing on his console.

"Where have you been, Frankie?" she said, tapping her watch.

"Sorry!" said Frankie. "I lost track of time."

His mum smiled. "You and that football!"

Kevin looked up, narrowing his eyes. "Yes, you've been gone ages. Must have been quite a game?"

Frankie was glad it was dark so his brother couldn't see him blush.

"Do you want me to cook you a burger?" asked his mum.

Frankie patted his stomach. He was still full, and anyway, he doubted anything could compare with the burger on the space station. "Actually, I'm not that hungry. Where's Dad?"

"He's in the clearing behind the

cabin," said Kevin. "Messing with that telescope."

Frankie walked around the side of the cabin, and found his father with his eye to the telescope. It rested in its tripod, pointing up through the trees. Stars twinkled in an almost cloudless sky.

"Hey, Dad!" said Frankie.

His dad glanced at him, then frowned. "What's that?" he asked, pointing at Frankie's chest.

Frankie looked down and saw a gleaming golden disc pinned to his shirt. The Cadet Medal! Somehow, it had magicked its way to Frankie. He glanced at Max, and noticed that he now had a medal on his collar. Charlie and Louise must have got theirs too!

"Er . . . it's just a badge from school," he muttered. He pointed upwards. "Seen anything good?"

"The stars are incredible," said his dad. "You missed the meteor shower, though!"

Oh no, I didn't, Frankie wanted to say.

He clutched the ball tightly to his chest, and gazed up at the night sky. It was good to know that he'd rescued his new friends from a meteor.

"Come and look at the stars,"

his dad said, stepping away from the telescope. Frankie handed his football over and peered through the eye piece. Far above him, he could see the stars and planets so close he could almost touch them. Almost ... He wondered if he'd ever play football in zero gravity again!

ACKNOWLEDGEMENTS

Many thanks to everyone at Hachette Children's Group; Neil Blair, Zoe King, Daniel Teweles and all at The Blair Partnership; Luella Wright for bringing my characters to life; special thanks to Michael Ford for all his wisdom and patience; and to Steve Kutner for being a great friend and for all his help and guidance, not just with the book but with everything.

Read on for an exclusive extract from Frankie's next adventure, *The Great Santa Race*, coming soon!

It's almost Christmas, and Frankie and his friends are gathered to watch Frankie's neighbour, Mr Harris, turn on his impressive display of Christmas lights ...

"OK, countdown from three!" called Mr Harris. He was standing by a switch just inside his garage side-door.

Frankie joined in the count. *"Three! Two! One!"*

Mr Harris flicked the switch and the lights all came on together. The crowd gasped. The penguins all glittered with white spots like snow crystals. The front of the house came alive with stars. Most impressive of all was the Santa on the garage. The lights were blinking off and on along the sled, making it appear to shoot through the air. A red light flashed on Rudolph's nose, and white pulses of light from Santa's mouth looked like breath misting on a cold night.

Suddenly, Frankie felt his football being snatched from under his arm.

"Give it back, Kev," said Frankie. He looked around nervously. The last thing he needed was the football's magic kicking in while people were watching.

Kevin glanced past Frankie's head. "Reckon I can kick it over our roof?" he asked.

"No!" said Frankie and all his friends together.

Kevin grinned, tossed the ball in the air and kicked it in a high arc towards the house. For a second, Frankie thought it would make it. But at the top of its loop, a gust seemed to catch the ball. It bounced on to the tiles, then fell back down. With his heart in his mouth, Frankie watched the ball fall, fall, fall — right towards the penguins in Mr Harris's front garden.

Crash!

The ball thumped into the largest penguin's head, knocking it over. A shower of sparks sprayed up from the fallen creature.

One by one, all the lights in the garden and across the house blinked out until Frankie was stood in pitch black.

There was complete silence. Frankie could just see Charlie's mouth hanging open. A cold wind blew across the front of the houses, and Louise let out a "Brrrrrr!".

"What have you done?" screeched Mr Harris. He was standing by his model penguins, hands clutching his hair in the moonlight. "My display!" Then his eyes fell on the football. "You!" he said, pointing a trembling finger at Frankie. "You've ruined everything!"

Competition Time

COULD YOU BE A WINNER LIKE FRANKIE?

Every month one lucky fan will win an exclusive
Frankie's Magic Football goodie bag! Here's how to enter:

Every **Frankie's Magic Football** book
features different animals. Go to:
www.frankiesmagicfootball.co.uk/competitions
and name three different animals that feature in three
different **Frankie's Magic Football** books.
Then you could be a winner!

You can also send your entry by post by filling in
the form on the opposite page.

Once complete, please send your entries to:

Frankie's Magic Football Competition
Hachette Children's Books, Carmelite House,
50 Victoria Embankment,
London, EC4Y 0DZ

GOOD LUCK!

Competition Entry Page

Please enter your details below:

1. Name of Frankie Book: ....
        Animal: ....

2. Name of Frankie Book: ....
        Animal: ....

3. Name of Frankie Book: ....
        Animal: ....

My name is: ....
My date of birth is: ....
Email address: ....
Address 1: ....
Address 2: ....
Address 3: ....
County: ....
Post Code: ....

Parent/Guardian signature: ....

FRANKIE'S MAGIC FOOTBALL WEBSITE

Have you had a chance to check out **frankiesmagicfootball.co.uk** yet?

Get involved in **competitions**, find out **news** and updates about the series, play **games** and watch **videos** featuring the author, **Frank Lampard!**

Visit the site to join **Frankie's FC** today!